Molly the Muffin Fairy

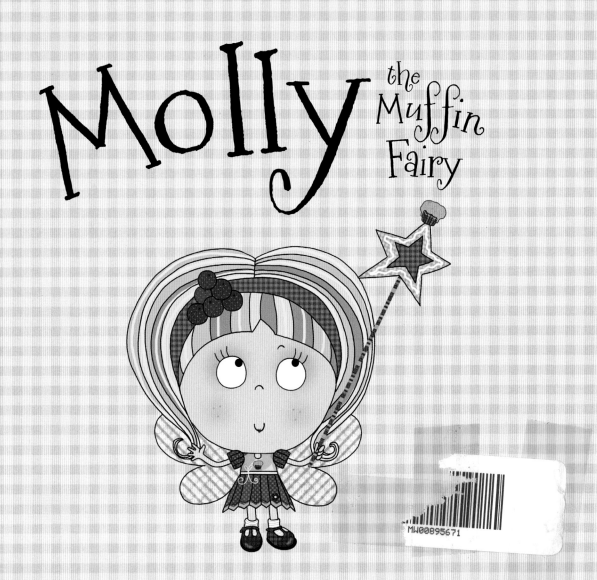

Tim Bugbird · Lara Ede

make
believe
ideas

MW00895671

Molly the Muffin Fairy was famous in Fairyland for making perfect muffins — some small and some quite grand.

Each one was baked 'til **spongy**,
golden, soft, and sweet.
Her wand put in big **blueberries**
to make the **treats** complete!

The blueberries came in boxes, delivered by Mel and Kerri, her two **best friends**, who drove a truck shaped like a **giant berry!**

But then one day when baking,
Molly's temper began to fray;

her muffins had no softness —
she was having a bad bake day!

Her baking got **no better**,

and soon **Molly's** fairy home

was full of **rubbery muffins**

with tops as hard as **stone!**

Molly was not happy. The baking was making her MAD!

She fussed and fumed and finally flipped!

What she did was really bad . . .

She grabbed a tray of muffins and threw them to the floor,
then took a muffin in her hand and hurled it out the door!

The muffin hit her trampoline and bounced up in the air.

The strangest scene there's **ever** been **followed** on from there . . .

and pinged
and ponged,

It bounced
and bumped

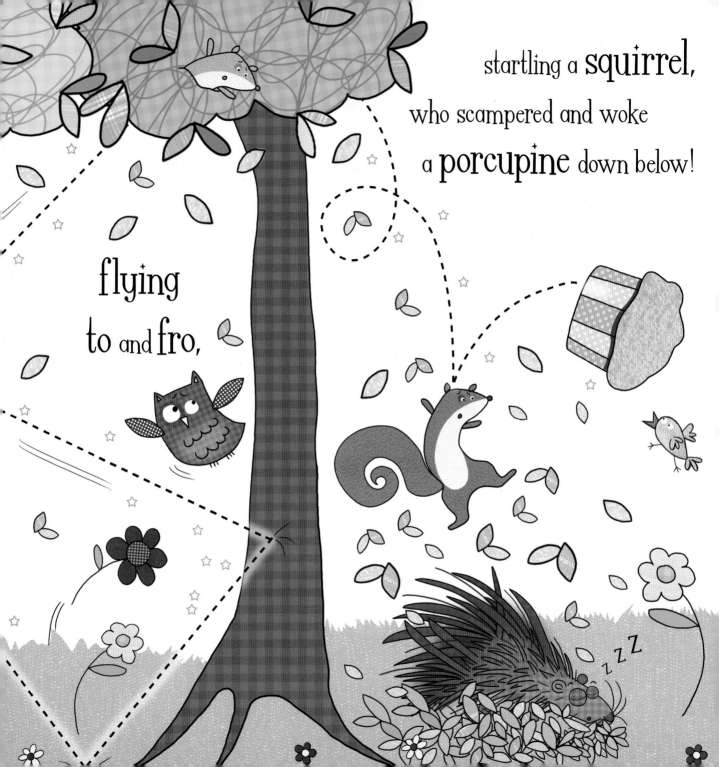

startling a **squirrel,**
who scampered and woke
a **porcupine** down below!

flying
to and **fro,**

zzz

Up with a **start**, the porcupine **ran**
to find a **safe place** to hide.

But he poked the edge of Molly's pool —
his spikes making holes in the side!

Water gushed out from the holes,
flooding the road all around.

Then Mel and Kerri's truck arrived, but how would they cross the wet ground?

Molly cried, "It's all a mess!"
Mel said, "Oh, stop whining!
Those muffins of yours could help us —
every cloud has a silver lining!"

"Maybe they could make a **path**. Just try and see."
So **Molly** laid the **muffins** down . . .

and the truck

crossed **easily!**

Then, before the fairies' eyes,
the muffins began to expand.

Soaking up water, they became
the **biggest** in Fairyland!

"The muffins feel soft!" cried Molly.

"Don't eat them, though; they're not clean!

But squashed together, I think they'll make . . ."

Molly learned that when things look bad, you can always find a way to see things from the **sunny side** and turn around your day!

Camilla
the Cupcake Fairy

Tim Bugbird • Lara Ede

make
believe
ideas

On **Camilla's** fifth birthday,
the Pink Fairy Post
sent to Camilla what she **dreamed** of most.

Not a **hat**, or a **doll**, or a **plant** in a pot,
or anything else she'd already got.

She **tore** off the paper and **giggled** with glee.
"A **wand!**" cried Camilla. "And meant just for **me!**"

It was so very shiny and sparkly and new.
Her very first wand! But **what** would it **do?**

If she waved it carefully
and closed her eyes tight,

could she wish for a party
with dancing all night?

Or if she sat nicely, not making a noise,

would it make her bed neatly and put away toys?

Or would it put on a show
with a dancing dog,

The answer was no!

But what it would make,

Camilla was told, was

frosting for cake!

So she found a plain cupcake,

which she placed by her feet,

her wand at the ready,

to make a pink treat!

And holding the **wand**, Camilla stood straight.

She took a deep breath
but just **could**
not
wait . . .

She waved it so fast,
the wand would not stop
whirling and twirling
and flashing on top!

It jumped and it jerked,
with a rattle and a shake,
it jiggled and it juddered
'til she thought
it would break!

Then, with a **BANG**,
bright stars filled the air.

She looked for
sweet frosting,
but the cupcake was bare!

And there on the **top**,
not making a sound,
was a tiny white
mouse,
with eyes bright
and **round**!

So she started again, this time taking care
to wave the wand gently. But look what was there!

Covering the cake where

the frosting should be . . .

So she tried one more **wave**, not too **fast** or too **slow**.

Now topping the cake there was nothing but . . . **snow!**

Well, snowballs and snowmen
she didn't much mind,
but this fancy frosting
was just the
wrong kind!

"Oh dear," thought Camilla.

"This just isn't right.

My wand is not working,

I'll be here all night!"

But then, when it seemed she was down on her luck,

Ms. Sprinkles drove by in her pink fairy truck.

Camilla asked nicely, "What should I do?"

Her teacher said kindly, "I'll give you a clue!"

"Working alone is never much fun,
but with help from your friends, the job is soon done!"

So she called her **friends** on her pink $fairy$ phone.

Molly and Maya were glad to be home.

Said Molly to Maya,
"Our friend's in a state!

Let's fly to Camilla,

this problem

won't wait!"

They held the **wand** steady
with eyes closed tight.

As they worked hard together,
it shone a **bright** light.

Then crossing their fingers
in a shower of gold **twinkles**,
they all **wished** together
for frosting and
sprinkles!

All of a sudden,
the fairy friends found
the tastiest treat,
just there on the ground.

With sparkling
sprinkles
and frosting
so sweet,

the best-ever
cupcake
was right at their feet!

So the **wand** could work wonders, but nothing compared to the gift of **true friendship** the three **fairies** shared!

This book belongs to
....

Lola the Lollipop Fairy

Tim Bugbird · Lara Ede

make
believe
ideas

Once upon a time
in a circus big top,
lived a fairy family,
the sisters Lollipop!

Every day at **six o'clock**,
come rain or shine or snow,
fairies came from **far** and **wide**
to see their famous show!

Show
~~~~~~
6pm

Lola was the one in charge

and Linda lifted weights.

Lulu juggled lollipops
and sometimes spinning plates!

Their act had been the same for years
and their tent was worn and old,
but every night they did their best
and all the seats were sold.

'Til one morning Lola woke;
she yawned and rubbed her eyes.
She looked outside and had a shock -
what a bad surprise!

Next door, where the grass had been,

the plants and trees and flowers,

there stood a brand-new theme park

with rides and slides and towers!

cat bed

The park became
the **place to go**,
where fairies met to play,
and **no one**
came to Lola's show.
She sighed, as if to say,
"The rides are so exciting,
we just cannot **compete**."
Lulu said, "Let's face it, friends,
I think we might be **beat**!"

"So we'll just make our show **better!**"
Lola boldly cried.
"We'll do our **best**, so if we fail,
at least we'll know we tried!"

"Let's think of something **super big**, a **spectacular** creation, a show to make the fairies talk — **we'll** be the new **sensation!**"

In a flash it came to Lola —
a plan to make them swoon.
Lola the Fairy Cannonball
would fly up to the moon!

ideas box

So the fairies built a **cannon**
that was just the perfect size
to fire fearless **Lola**
from the circus to the skies!
They **banged** and **bashed**,
and **clanged** and **clashed**
until the job was done.
The work was **hard**,
the hours were **long**,
but they'd never had **such fun**!

The day for launching Lola
came around really fast.
Linda hollered, "Three, two, one!"
and, with a deafening BLAST,

Lola shot up into space
as the fairies waved and cheered.
And Lola thought, "What a lovely place,
I'm glad I volunteered!"

And when Lola finally landed, she cried:
"Oh my goodness, golly!
I thought the moon was made of cheese,
but it's a great big orange lolly!"

It certainly was the sweetest place
Lola had ever seen,
with lollipops of every kind
and mountains of whipped cream!

The **air** was
sweet as **strawberries**
and the **sky** was
pink and **clear**.
Lola flew back down to earth —
she'd had a **new idea**.

Her cannon show had been a blast,

but this plan was the ace.

They'd make their fairy fortunes

firing fairies into space!

And so the sisters got to work, they never seemed to stop.

Soon the moon trips made enough to buy a

new BIG TOP!

With a brand-new sparkly cannon, glitter and lights aglow,
very soon the stage was set for their amazing circus show!

It was **thrilling** and **exciting**, a full house **every night**.
The fairies **saved the circus** thanks to Lola's **daring flight**!

So Lola, Linda, and Lulu made the perfect team.

By working hard, and not giving up, they lived their fairy dream!

Izzy ^the Ice-cream Fairy

Tim Bugbird · Lara Ede

make
believe
ideas

Once upon a time,
in a **sunny**, sandy land,
lived Izzy, Mo, and Mia
at a pretty ice-cream stand.

The fairy friends
scooped ice cream
from their famous ice-cream well
to sell in rainbow flavors, in a crispy wafer shell.

And for a **treat**, their fairy wands sent **showers**, in all **directions**,

of candy jewels
and chocolate chips,
to top the iced
confections.

They saved up EVERY penny
to fund their carnival float

and every year, for Best in Show,
they won the fairies' vote!

Then, early one summer,
they peered inside their well,
expecting flowing ice cream,
but there was nothing
left to sell!

The well had run **completely** dry. **Why?** They had no clue.

But being **modern** fairies, they **knew** just what to do!

Izzy surfed the fairynet for places cold and chilly with ice cream in abundance, but the results were just too silly!

If you said them fast enough, they sounded almost right, but two made Izzy laugh out loud, and one was just a fright!

"Where can I find **ice cream**?" Tap, tap, tap . . .

"No, that's not right!"

"No, that's not right!"

"**No!**
That's definitely
not right!"

Tap, tap, tap . . . 🔍 ICE CREAM

"Yes!"

Izzy finally found a place
with no palms, sea, or sand.
It was **far away** but perfect –
she'd discovered Ice-cream Land!

Without delay,

the friends took flight

to a place of ice-cream mountains,

with sprinkles falling from the sky

and fruit-filled,

syrup fountains!

"Welcome to our magical land!" said Her Majesty the Queen.

"It's such a lovely place to live, but there's just too much ice cream!"

"You see, it covers everything, so things are getting lost. I'm sure my bike is somewhere here, buried in the frost!"

Izzy said, "That's funny,

our land is **warm** and **sunny**,

and since our ice-cream well ran dry,

we can't make any **money.**"

"Can we work **together**? This feels like such good **luck**."
"Grab a **shovel**," said the Queen, "and I'll call

RENT-A-TRUCK!"

They dug and dug
and dug
and dug,
until it was quite clear,
their ice-cream haul
would be enough
to last at least a year!

ICE 1

The journey **home** was **hampered** by fog and **long**, **dark** nights,

so Mo and Mia
lit their path
with **lanterns** and
fairy lights!

The trip took so **much longer**
than Izzy thought it would
and as they neared the **beach**, she cried,
"**Oh, no,** this isn't good!
The **carnival** starts today —
whatever will we ride?
It's way **too late** to make our float,
our hands are simply tied!"

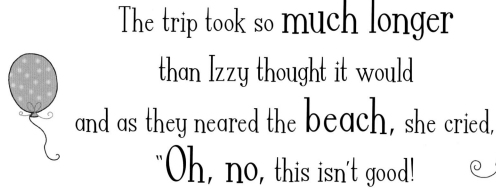

carnival today

But fortune had, for Izzy, one last **big surprise**:

all along the road ahead were floats of **every size!**

The fairies' truck joined the line, with its beautiful **glowing** lights.

It was just as good as a carnival float — a splendid, sparkling sight!

The fairies got to work,
serving ice cream to the crowd.
They made it home just in time
and had never felt so proud.

Their float did not win Best in Show,
but Izzy didn't mind,
for the love and joy that filled the day
was a prize of a better kind!

Izzy, Mo, and Mia made the perfect fairy team, and now they knew just who to call when they needed more ice cream!